# THE GHOST IN ANNIE'S ROOM

Philippa Pearce is one of the most popular children's book authors. Her books include the modern classics *Minnow on the Say*, *A Dog So Small* and *Tom's Midnight Garden* (for which she was awarded the Carnegie Medal). She also won the Whitbread Children's Book Award for *The Battle of Bubble and Squeak*. Many of her stories are based in or around the Cambridgeshire village where she was brought up and in which, after several years in London, she lives today.

Books by the same author

*Here Comes Tod!*

*Lion at School and Other Stories*

*The Battle of Bubble and Squeak*

For older readers

*Tom's Midnight Garden*

*A Dog So Small*

# PHILIPPA PEARCE

# The Ghost in Annie's Room

## Illustrations by Anthony Lewis

WALKER BOOKS
AND SUBSIDIARIES
LONDON • BOSTON • SYDNEY

First published 2001 by Walker Books Ltd
87 Vauxhall Walk, London SE11 5HJ

Published in hardback by Heinemann Library, a division of
Reed Educational and Professional Publishing Limited,
by arrangement with Walker Books Ltd

Based on the author's own story, of the same title,
first broadcast and published by the BBC
in their *Listening and Reading* series in 1980

2 4 6 8 10 9 7 5 3 1

Text © 2001 Philippa Pearce
Illustrations © 2001 Anthony Lewis

This book has been typeset in Garamond

Printed in Great Britain by
St Edmundsbury Press, Bury St Edmunds

British Library Cataloguing in Publication Data:
a catalogue record for this book
is available from the British Library

0-7445-5993-6 (paperback)
0-431-01790-5 (hardback)

# Contents

# Chapter One

At first Emma Brown liked the look of the little attic bedroom. Great-aunt Win said, "I thought you might like to sleep here, dear."

Emma said at once, "Oh, *yes!* Thank you!"

Emma and her brother, Joe, and their parents had come to stay for three nights with Great-aunt Win in her little cottage by the sea. There was not much room for visitors.

Joe was going to sleep downstairs
on a camp-bed. Mum and Dad
would sleep in the spare room
upstairs. And then there was the
attic bedroom at the very top of
the house…

"I'm so glad you like this bedroom, dear," said Great-aunt Win to Emma. "It's a little girl's room – *my* little girl's room." Great-aunt Win sighed. "Oh, I still miss Annie so!"

"Who's Annie?" asked Emma.

Mum was standing beside her at the top of the attic stairs. She frowned and said, "Really, Emma! You ought to know about your cousin Annie. She was your auntie Win's little girl, long ago."

"Oh," said Emma.

Later, downstairs, when the two children were alone, Joe said to Emma, "You're going to sleep in the haunted bedroom."

"Don't be stupid."

"I'm not being stupid. Dad and Mum were talking, and they didn't know I could hear. They said the attic bedroom was haunted, but the ghost wouldn't do you any harm, anyway, probably."

"I don't believe you," said Emma. "How could you overhear all that?"

"I just could."

"It's all rubbish," said Emma. "I'm going to ask Mum and Dad."

"Oh, yes, you do that! Of course, they'll say there isn't a ghost, just to comfort you."

So, after that, Emma did not ask about any ghost in the attic bedroom. Besides, as she told herself, Joe teased. Sometimes his teases were really bad, and she hated them. Like now.

But the main thing to remember was, there was no ghost.

# Chapter Two

That night Emma was the first to go to bed. Great-aunt Win took her up to her bedroom.

There was a door on the landing, by the other two bedrooms, and then a steep, narrow staircase led straight up into the attic. It was a little room right under the roof.

At the far end was a window.
A tree grew just outside. Its leaves
darkened the window and filled
the room with shadows. There was
a bed and a dressing-table with
a long mirror.

Great-aunt Win pointed out a
shelf full of little china ornaments.
"Annie's china cats and kittens, that
she collected when she was your
age. She doted on animals. Doted."
Great-aunt Win sighed. Emma
wished she wouldn't sigh every
time she mentioned Cousin Annie.

"Here's the light switch," Great-aunt Win said more briskly. "It's rather difficult to find in the dark, so notice it now. But you won't want to put it on, once you're in bed. You'll be so cosy up here. Annie always was. She loved it."

Great-aunt Win sighed again.

Mum came to tuck Emma up for the night. "Remember, Em, if you want us, you only have to come down the stairs. When I go down, I'll leave that stair door ajar. It will stay open all night."

"But I'll be all right up here, won't I?"

"Of course you will," said Mum. She kissed Emma goodnight, and left her.

Emma listened to the gentle rustling of leaves just outside the attic window. After a while, she fell asleep.

She woke with a start. It seemed
to be hours later. She was sure that
someone had been trying to wake
her by tapping at the window.
*Someone was tapping at the
window.*

She listened without moving.

The tapping sometimes stopped,
then started again. It always started
again.

And she was sure that there were eyes looking at her.

But through her fear she noticed another sound. A wind had risen and was blowing quite hard round the little house. It would be tossing the branches of the tree just outside her attic window. An idea came to her. She sat up in bed and looked towards the window.

Yes, she was right. The wind was rattling leaves and twigs against the glass. That was what had sounded like fingers tapping.

She lay back in bed. She forgot about eyes that had looked at her. She fell asleep.

By morning the wind had blown itself out; but at breakfast Joe said, "I bet the wind was howling round your bedroom last night, Em."

"Really?" said Emma, munching toast. "I slept. It's such a cosy room. I'm sorry about your camp-bed downstairs."

# Chapter Three

The blustery night was followed by a
day of perfect sunshine. The Brown
family spent all of it by the sea.

Emma was tired when she went
to bed.

"Sleep well," Mum said, as she
tucked her up.

But Emma lay awake. Suddenly
she thought of the door at the
bottom of the attic stairs. Had Mum
remembered to leave it open? Of
course, that really didn't matter,
now that there wasn't a ghost.

All the same…

31

Moonlight shone through the window, but there were shadows in certain corners of the room. Emma remembered last night's feeling of being watched, and wished she had not remembered it.

She made up her mind to get out of bed. She meant to put on the light and have a proper look round  the attic; but she could not find the light switch.

She decided to go down the attic stairs and check that the door was still open. She felt her way down, and – sure enough – it had been left ajar.

Through the gap she could even hear the TV from downstairs.

So that was all right.

She climbed the stairs again to go back to bed. As she began to cross the attic floor, she was looking towards the window.

*A dim figure in white was
coming towards her.*

It looked like a little girl. It paused, just as Emma halted. Emma tried to open her mouth to scream. She wanted to scream, but could not. It was like a nightmare. She could make no sound. But she raised her arm to protect herself. And, from under her arm, she saw that the figure in white also raised its arm, just as she was doing. Exactly like her.

Then Emma realized what she was looking at – her own reflection in the mirror of the dressing-table!

She watched herself watching herself in the mirror. Then she went back to bed. Oddly the feeling of watching eyes did not leave her; but she slept.

Next morning, she did not tell anyone of her midnight mistake. But she said to Joe, "No ghost again last night!"

He replied grumpily. "Oh, I just knew you'd believe anything!"

# Chapter Four

The Browns' second day by the sea was almost as good as the first. But towards the end of it, dark clouds built up on the horizon and thunder rumbled in the distance.

Great-aunt Win worried for Emma sleeping at the top of the house. "I hope you're not frightened by thunder and lightning, dear?"

Mum said, "Oh, Emma's all right, aren't you, Em? It's Joe who doesn't like it much."

Joe looked furious; Emma looked smug.

That night Emma heard the thunder coming closer through her dreams, and she woke to a flash of lightning.

She gave a little shriek, for someone really was standing in the middle of the floor. It was Mum: "I've only come up to shut the window against the rain."

So that was all right.

Emma listened to Mum's
footsteps going down the attic
stairs. Now Mum would be going
to check on Joe downstairs, to
make sure that he was all right. He
really hated thunder and lightning.

Thunder and lightning would not keep Emma awake. She settled herself to sleep again.

But she could not sleep.

Her feeling from the night before and from the night before that returned… *Someone was in the room, watching her.* This time she was certain of it.

"But there's no one," she said to herself.

Yet there must be.

She waited for the next flash of lightning. No one there.

Yet she was sure that eyes watched her.

She forced herself to sit up in bed. There was a lull in the storm: no thunder, no lightning. She peered into the attic's shadowy corners.

Then she saw the watcher: two
yellow eyes were staring at her
almost from floor level.

"Oh! It's a cat!" She called to it softly: "Puss, puss, puss!" But the little cat – very dark, with a white front – would not come to her. It slid away among the shadows, hardly more than a shadow itself.

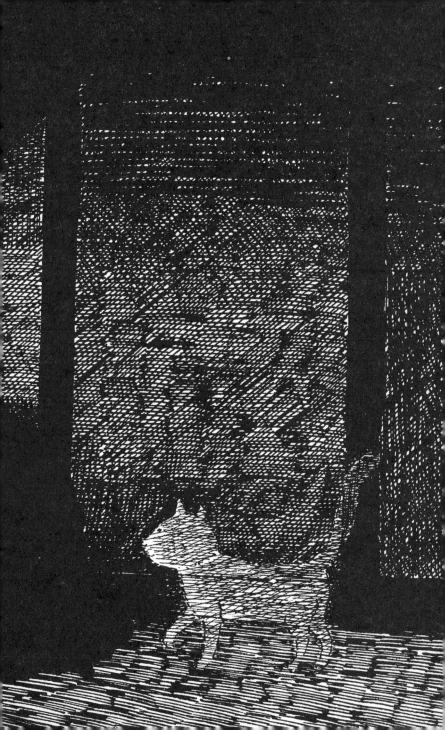

"Don't be afraid of the thunder and lightning," Emma whispered. "I'll look after you." Its eyes stared at her, but it would not come.

At last Emma gave up coaxing it. She lay down again to go to sleep. She wondered how the little cat had got up into the attic, but then remembered the door left ajar. That was it.

She was dozing off again, when she heard purring from the foot of the bed. The little cat had come to her after all. It had jumped on to her duvet…

She would have liked to press her feet against the cat for company, but she didn't want to frighten it away. It was such a timid little thing.

"Goodnight, puss," Emma whispered. She slept.

# Chapter Five

When Emma woke in the morning, the cat had gone.

At breakfast, Great-aunt Win asked if Emma had slept well.

"Very well, thank you, Auntie. I like Cousin Annie's room. Is she dead?"

"Emma!" cried Mum, shocked.

"Cousin Annie is married with five children, and she lives in New Zealand."

Great-aunt Win sighed. "I miss Annie so."

Emma made a face at Joe, but he pretended not to notice.

Later, in the car, going home, Emma said, "I wanted to say goodbye to the cat."

"What cat?" said Joe. "She hasn't a cat."

"The little black one with a white front. It slept all night on my bed."

"She hasn't a cat," repeated Joe.

"She has."

"She hasn't."

"Stop that," said Dad.

Mum had not been listening properly to the argument. Now she said quickly, "You're both right, in a way. Auntie hasn't a cat. But long ago, when Cousin Annie was a little girl, she had a little black cat with a white front. Auntie showed me a photo of them together. And ...

she said the cat always slept at the
bottom of Annie's bed. Just as you
said, Emma."